Discover Series
MASCOTAS

Gato

Chinchilla

Perro

Rana

Pez de Colores

Pinzón de Gould

Conejillo de Indias

Hámster

Cangrejo Ermitaño

Caballo

Ratoncito de Casa

Gatito

Lagartija

Ratoncito

Tritón

Perico

Loro

Poni

Cachorro

Conejo

Ratón

Serpiente

Tortuga

Tortuga

Make Sure to Check Out the Other Discover Series Books from Xist Publishing:

Published in the United States by Xist Publishing
www.xistpublishing.com
PO Box 61593 Irvine, CA 92602

© 2012 by Xist Publishing
© 2018 Spanish Copyright Xist Publishing
Translated by Victor Santana
First Spanish Edition   All rights reserved
No portion of this book may be reproduced without express permission of the publisher
All images licensed from Fotolia
ISBN: 978-1-53240-723-9 eISBN: 978-1-53240-724-6

www.ingramcontent.com/pod-product-compliance
Lightning Source LLC
LaVergne TN
LVHW070950070426
835507LV00030B/3480